BIG BOOK OF ABCs AND 123s

ELMO

RP | KIDS
PHILADELPHIA

"ABCs with Elmo and Friends" was originally published as *ABC Fun with Elmo and Friends* by Flying Frog Publishing. Copyright © 2007 Sesame Workshop.

"The Twiddlebug Alphabet" was originally published as *Sesame Street ABCs Twiddlebug Alphabet* by Sesame Workshop. Copyright © 2010 Sesame Workshop.

"Grover's Own Alphabet" was originally published as *Grover's Own Alphabet* by Random House Children's Books. Copyright © 1993 Sesame Workshop.

"The ABCs of Cookies!" was originally published as *The ABCs of Cookies* by International Masters Publishers, Inc. Copyright © 2011 Sesame Workshop.

"Animal ABCs" was originally published as *Animal Alphabet* by International Masters Publishers, Inc. Copyright © 2010 Sesame Workshop.

"Elmo's Alphabet Soup" was originally published as *Elmo's Alphabet Soup* by Random House Children's Books. Copyright © 2011 Sesame Workshop.

"Storybook ABCs with Elmo and Friends" was originally published as *Storybook ABCs* by Dalmatian Press, LLC. Copyright © 2013, 2008 Sesame Workshop.

"Elmo's ABC Tricky Tongue Twisters" was originally published as *Elmo's Tricky Tongue Twisters* by Random House. Copyright © 1998 Sesame Workshop.

"Let's Count to 10!" was originally published as *Count to 10* by Dalmatian Press, LLC. Copyright © 2009, 1986 Sesame Workshop.

"1,2,3 Count with Me!" was originally published as *1,2,3 Count with Me* by Random House Children's Books. Copyright © 2005 Sesame Workshop.

"Learn to Count with Elmo" was originally published as *Sing & Learn Counting* by Publications International, Ltd. Copyright © 2008 Sesame Workshop.

"Rhyme and Count on Sesame Street" was originally published as *Over on Sesame Street: A Counting Rhyme* by Random House Children's Books. Copyright © 2012 Sesame Workshop.

"Counting All Around" was originally published as *Counting All Around* by International Masters Publishers, Inc. Copyright © 2010, 2005 Sesame Workshop.

"The Count's Castle" was originally published as *The Count's Castle* by International Masters Publishes, Inc. Copyright © 2010, 2009, 2001 Sesame Workshop.

Running Press Kids
Hachette Book Group
1290 Avenue of the Americas, New York, NY 10104
www.runningpress.com/rpkids
@RP_Kids

www.sesamestreet.org

Printed in China

First Edition: January 2018

Published by Running Press Kids, an imprint of Perseus Books, LLC, a subsidiary of Hachette Book Group, Inc.

The Hachette Speakers Bureau provides a wide range of authors for speaking events. To find out more, go to www.hachettespeakersbureau.com or call (866) 376-6591.

The publisher is not responsible for websites (or their content) that are not owned by the publisher.

Print book cover and interior design by Frances J. Soo Ping Chow.

Library of Congress Control Number: 2017935744

ISBN: 978-0-7624-6222-3 (hardcover)

1010

10 9 8 7 6 5 4 3 2 1

TABLE OF CONTENTS

ABCs

WITH ELMO AND FRIENDS

Hi, everybody! Are you ready to say the alphabet with Elmo? Come on, let's go.

ant

book

Cc

Dd

Ee

cookie

dog

egg

Ff

firefighter

hat

Hh

Gg

goat

Ii

igloo

Jj

jam

What's your favorite flavor of jam?

kite

Kk

Mm

Ll

lion

magician

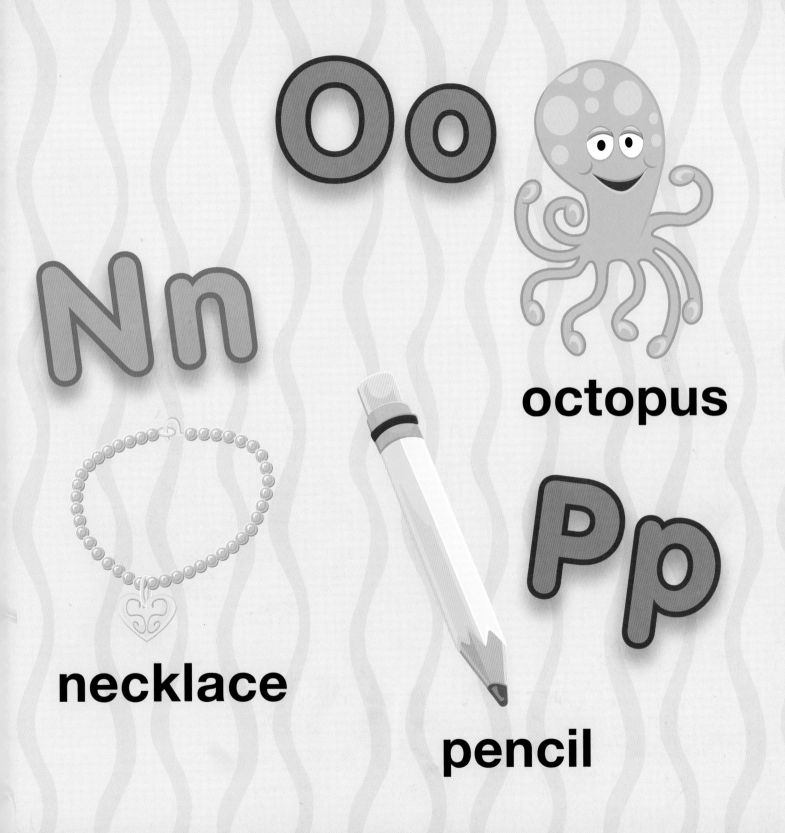

Nn

Oo

octopus

necklace

Pp

pencil

Qq

quilt

Rr

rake

Ss

sun

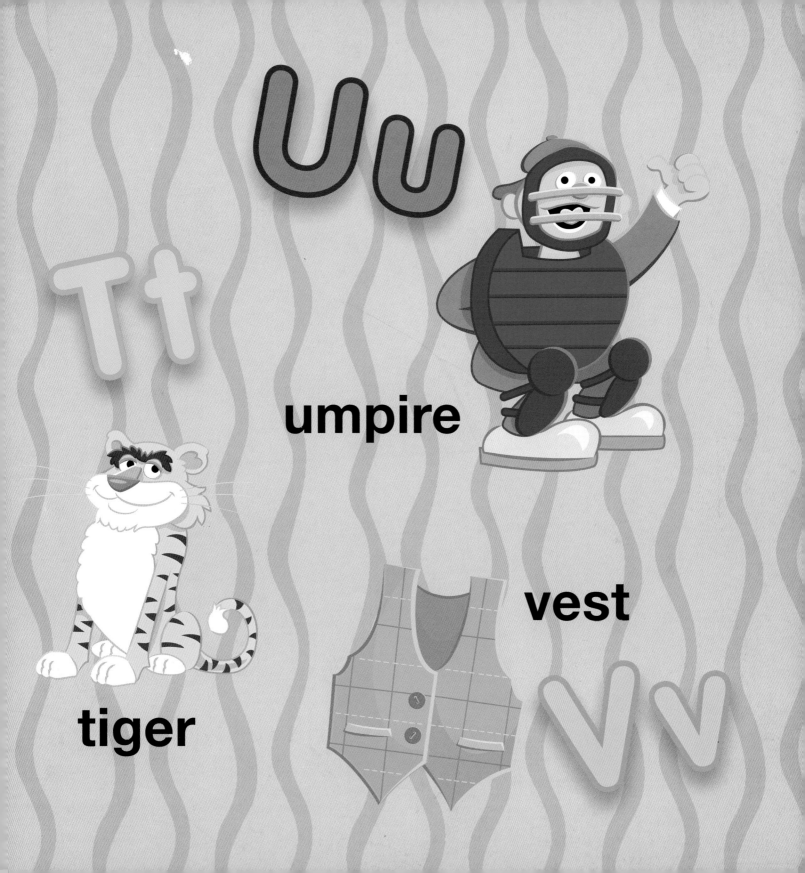

Uu

Tt

umpire

tiger

vest

Vv

W w

worm

Y y

yarn

X x

x-ray

Zz

Zipper

That was great! Now you can sing the alphabet!

THE TWIDDLEBUG ALPHABET

astronaut

ball

cookie

dog

elephant

fish

grapes

hat

insects

jacket

kite

lobster

moose

noodles

ostriches

pants

quilt

raccoon

soap

turtle

umbrella

vegetables

whale

xylophone

yogurt

zebra

GROVER'S OWN ALPHABET

This is a little awkward, but is it not an absolutely adorable **A**?

I bet you think making this big, beautiful B with
my furry little body is easy.
Well, it is not!

And now I am making you a *cute* letter C!
But I am not very comfortable.

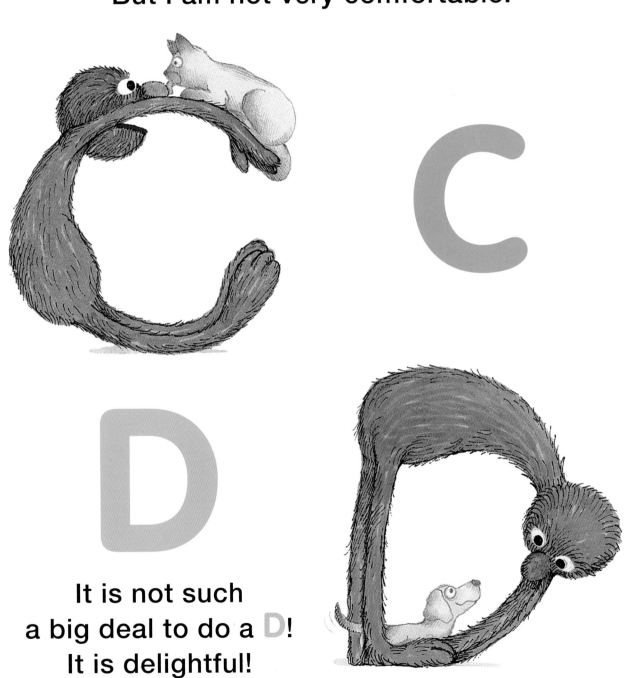

C

D

It is not such
a big deal to do a D!
It is delightful!

I have to bend my elbow exactly right,
but how is this for an elegant E? EEEK!

Here is a funny, furry **F** for you!

G is for GROVER! Watch while I, Grover,
form the great letter G! Am I not graceful?

I hope this H makes you happy.
It is hard to do (*pant, pant*). Help!

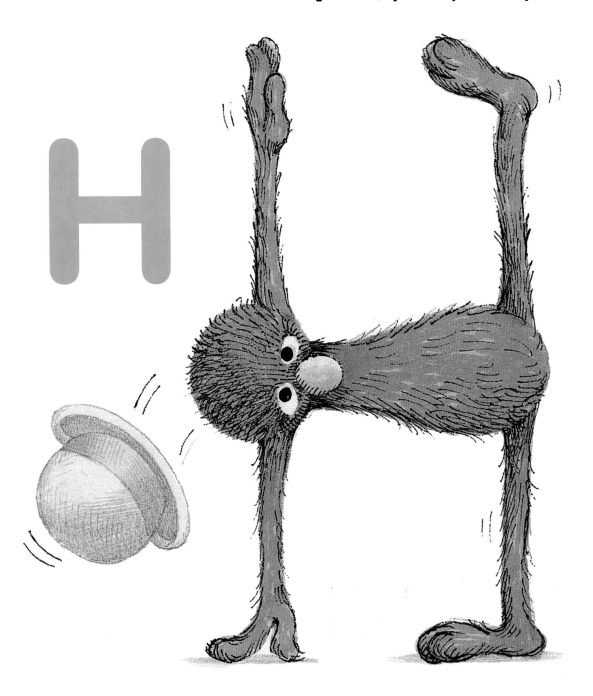

It is I, Grover, making the important letter I.

I

J

Now (*puff, puff*) I am juggling just to show you a J. I could get in a jam this way.

This is the letter K. I am not kidding.

K

I do not like to be lazy
about this, but the lovely letter L
takes very little work.

Isn't this a magnificent M?
It is made by ME!

I thought we would never get
to the nifty letter N!

Oh, my goodness (*glub, glub*)! I am not
the only one in this ocean.

What is the point of my standing like this?
I am pretending to be the letter P

Quick! Answer this question!
What letter am I now? Q? Oh, thank goodness
you guessed it.

You want an **R**? All *right!!* Here you are (*pant, pant*). This is getting ridiculous

So sorry. I couldn't find a single thing
to assist me with this S. I simply
had to use my *self*.

I have tried to make a *terrific* T for you!
But, oh, I am so tired. TA-DA!

U

I would undergo anything to show
you the letter **U**.

You are invited to view
my very valuable letter V.

I wish you would watch
my wonderful diving W!

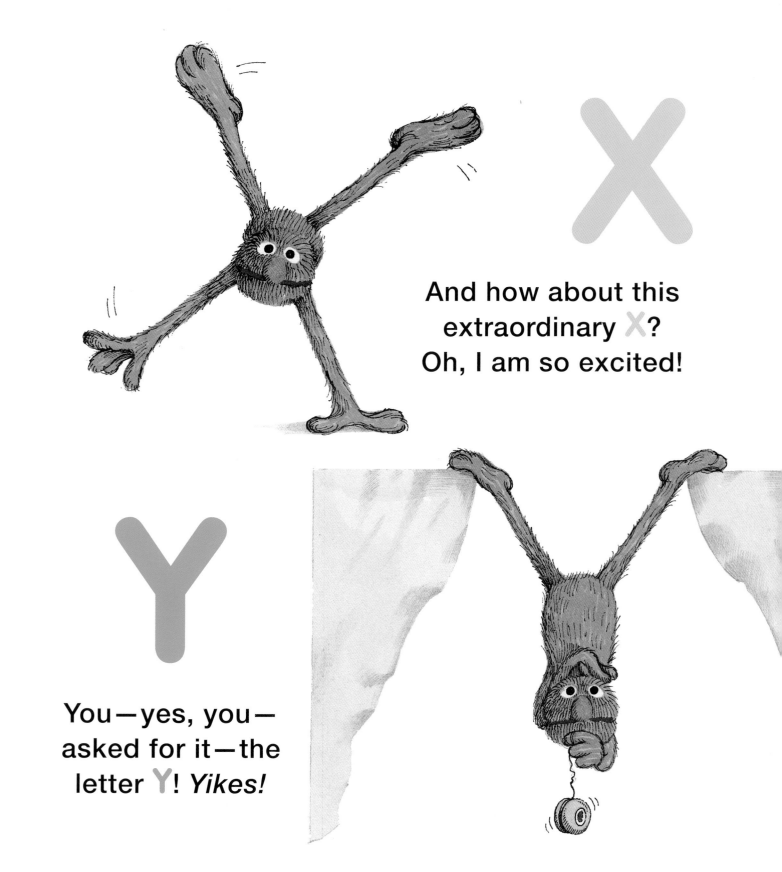

And how about this
extraordinary X?
Oh, I am so excited!

You—yes, you—
asked for it—the
letter Y! *Yikes!*

Here it is (*puff, puff*)—the last letter—Z!
Did you like the way I zipped through
the entire alphabet?

This is not a letter of the alphabet.
This is a tired monster!

THE ABCS OF COOKIES!

A is for apron, which matches this hat.

B is for butter, and . . .

D is for dishes.

E is for eggs, and . . .

F is for flour.

H is for **honey**.

K is for krispies you put on top.

L is for lemon juice.

N is for nutmeg.

O is for oven.

P is for pan. (But first put your gloves on!)

R is for raisins, golden and sweet.

S is for sprinkles.
And now . . .

Time to eat!

U-m-m-m is the way
a warm cookie tastes.

W is whipped cream to swirl on the top.
Or give a quick squeeze and then . . .

X marks the spot!

ANIMAL ABCs

Aa

Elmo is ready to learn the Animal Alphabet,
from ape to zebra!
Can you guess what animal
begins with A?
That's right, ape begins with A!

Ant also
begins with A!

Cc

Camel begins with C.
Canary and cat also begin with C.

Dd

Dog begins with D.
Duck begins with D, too.

Gg

Giraffe **and** grasshopper **begin with G.**

And don't forget goldfish!

Hh

Hippopotamus begins with H.

That's a very big word for a very big animal!

Ii iguana begins with i.

Jj Jaguar begins with J.

Kk

Kangaroo and koala begin with K.

Ll

Llama, ladybug, and lizard all begin with L.

Mm

Monkey begins with M.
Elmo loves monkeys!

Nn
Nightingale begins with N.

Oo
Owl begins with O.

Birds of a feather flock together!

Pp

Pigeon begins with P.
And pig begins with P, too.

Qq
Quail begins with Q.

Rr
Rabbit begins with R.

Tt Toucan begins with T.

Ww

Worm begins with W.

We grouches love **worms!**

Yy Yak begins with Y.

Zz Can you guess what animal
begins with Z?
That's right! Zebra
begins with Z!
And a zebu does, too.

Let's go through
this alphabet again.
Back to the ape!

ELMO'S ALPHABET SOUP

Elmo and Cookie Monster are making alphabet soup. Elmo wants it to have lots of tasty and healthy vegetables.

So what will they put into the pot?

Soup will be DEEEE-LI-CIOUS!

APPLE
Apple is a fruit!

BROCCOLI
Belongs.

CARROTS, CORN, CABBAGE
Lots of vegetables begin with C.

HERBS
  A heaping spoonful for flavor.

    ICE CREAM
      It's not for soup! It's *dessert!*

    JAM
        A spoonful on toast or oatmeal.

RADISH
Reserve for salad.

STRING BEANS
Super soup stuff!

TOMATOES
Tasty—throw them in.

UGLI FRUIT
No!

VEGETABLES
So many in vegetable soup!

WATER
What makes soup soupy!

XYLOPHONE
How silly!

YAM
Yes. Yummy!

ZUCCHINI
Yes. And that's the end
of the alphabet!

STORYBOOK ABCs WITH ELMO AND FRIENDS

A
Apple

Abby, Abby, quite Cadabby,
How does your alphabet grow?
With ABC—then letters to Z!
Twenty-six, all in a row.

The alphabet is amazing!

D
Dog

Hey, diddle-diddle,
The cat and the fiddle,
The cow jumped over the mooooon.
The little dog laughed to see such sport,
And the dish ran away with the spoon.

J
Jack

Jog and juggle! Jack, be quick!
Jack, jump over the candlestick!

Enough jogging, juggling, and jumping. I, Jack, am going back to beanstalks.

Old King Cole was a grouchy old soul,
And a grouchy old soul was he.
He called for some junk,
And he called for his skunk,
And he called his kazoo-players three.

K
King

L
Lamb

Prairie had a little lamb,
Little lamb, little lamb.
Prairie had a little lamb.
Its fleece was light as snow.

Messy Miss Muffet
Sat on a tuffet,
Eating some mud soufflé.
In marched a spider
To sit down beside her—
But she frightened that spider away!

O
Oven

P
Pie

Pat a pie, pat a pie, baker's man.
Make me a pie as fast as you can.
Pat it and prick it and mark it with P.
Put it in the oven for piggy and me!

Q

Queen

Oh, I quit.

The Queen of Hearts
Made quiche and tarts,
All on a quiet day.
The Knave of Hearts,
He stole those tarts
And quickly ran away!

ELMO'S ABC TRICKY TONGUE TWISTERS

Grover gobbles grapes as he gazes at gray
geese in the green grass.

Selling seashells by the seashore,
Snuffy got stuck in his seashell shop.

Baker Betty Lou bought some butter,
But it made her batter bitter.
So Baker Betty Lou bought some better butter
To make her bitter batter better.

Farley flips five fine flapjacks.

Mumford's in a fix doing tricks with six silly sticks.

Big Bird wants to teach Bert
to begin to toboggan.
But the toboggan Big Bird
brought Bert is too big.

Twelve Twiddlebugs twirl
twelve twisted twigs.

Elmo sits serenely and soaks in
sweet-smelling soapsuds.

Mushy bananas!
To munch the bunch would be too
much lunch.
Do you munch much mush for lunch?

Herry carried cherished chairs very carefully down the stairs.

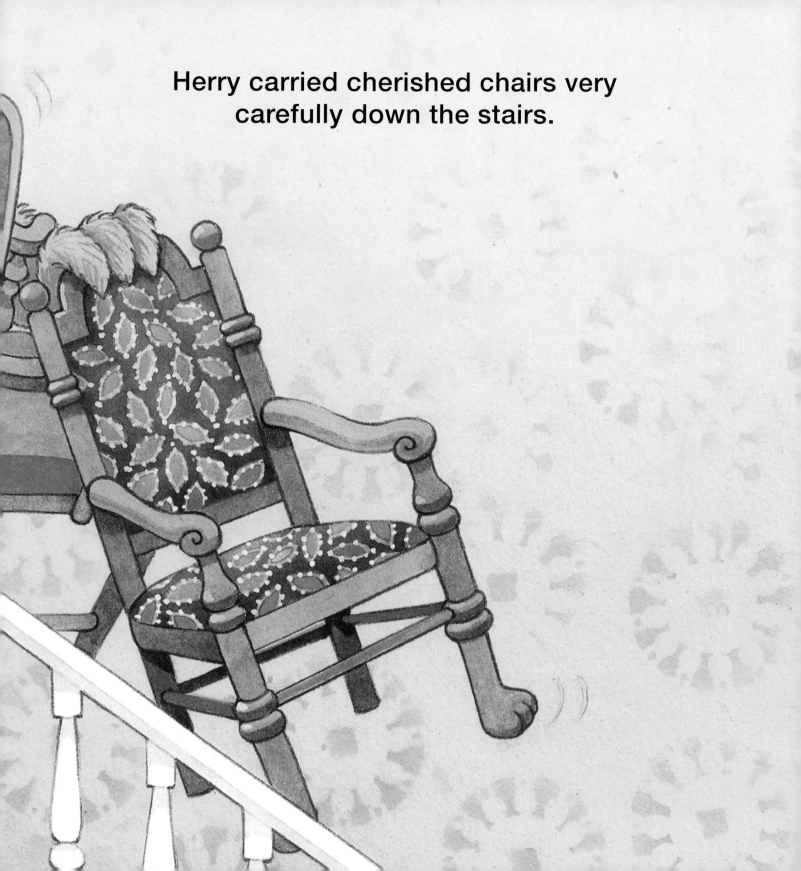

Oscar makes noise that annoys the boisterous oysters.

Hoots tried to tutor two tooters
To toot on a sax and a flute.
The two tooters asked Hoots,
"Is it harder to toot or
To tutor two tooters to toot?"

Ernie can't avert squirting Bert's shirt
with dessert.

Monster sisters insist on twisting.
Hope those sisters don't get blisters.

Sherry sure hopes she'll see the sun shine soon.

Did you like this silly book?
Then have some fellow tell it again while
Elmo plays cello for some swell, bellowing
yellow elephants.

LET'S COUNT TO 10!

1 One tire . . .

. . . makes a swing.

2 Two pieces of bread . . .

. . . make a sandwich.

3 Three snowballs . . .

. . . make a snowman.

4 Four letters . . .

. . . make Elmo's name.

5 Five musicians...

. . . make
a jazzy band.

6 **Six friends make a pyramid.**

7 **Seven stars make the Big Dipper.**

8 Eight patches . . .

. . . make Elmo's quilt.

9 **Nine baseball players
make a team.**

10 Ten
monsters . . .

...make a mess!

1, 2, 3 COUNT WITH ME!

Here comes...

1 big, gray elephant

2 striped tigers

3 proud peacocks

4 waddling penguins

5 slow turtles

6 golden lions

7 noisy parrots

8 jumping monkeys

9 prancing horses

10 friendly dogs

How many animals do you see?
Count them! Ready? 1, 2, 3...

LEARN TO COUNT WITH ELMO

1

Count with Elmo,
    Count with Elmo,
We'll start by Big Bird's nest.
    Count one ball, one tennis racket,
Then help Snuffy count the rest.

2

Monsters dancing,
  Monsters prancing,
Zoe and Elmo, that makes **two**.
  Count **two** dancers on the poster,
Two pink slippers, **two** tutus.

3

Super Grover
   Flies right over
The street called Sesame.
   Over cars and birds and street lamps
All of which, he counts **three**.

4

In a trash can,
   In a trash can,
Oscar counts four yellow peels.
   He counts four worms and four old tires,
Four roller blades each with four wheels.

5

Bert and Ernie
  Have a picnic
Let's count what they have to eat:
  Five sandwiches and fresh corn cobs,
And some fruit for something sweet.

6

Who could there be
  But a fairy
Magically counting to **six**?
  Count six broccoli and **six** flowers,
And **six** pumpkins, just for kicks.

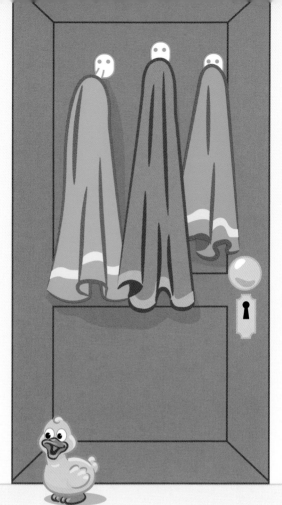

7

Splishy splashy,
　　Bubble bathy,
Ernie scrubs until he's clean.
　　Count with Ernie up to **seven**
All the bath things he has seen.

8

Cookie Monster,
   Cookie Monster,
He ate everything he could.
   Ate **eight** carrots and **eight** oranges,
And **eight** cookies, mmm! So good!

9

Time for school,
　Oh, how cool!
Elmo learns with Prairie Dawn.
　There are **nine** blocks and **nine** toy cars,
Nine books and **nine** crayons.

10

Candles dripping,
    Bat wings flipping,
Organ music plays along.
    Count **ten** bats, **ten** cats and spiders,
One through **ten**, our counting's done.

RHYME AND COUNT ON SESAME STREET

It's an apple-picking party and everyone's invited.
All the friends on Sesame Street are happy and excited.

1 merry monster is already on his way.
"Time for apples!" Elmo shouts,
then adds **1** loud "Hooray!"

2 grumpy grouches pop up with a crash, counting **2** old apple cores and other yucchy trash.

3 playful puppies pounce on Grover. They're not shy.
He counts those **3** and hurries on 'cause he
wants apple pie!

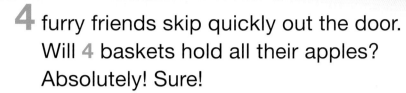

4 furry friends skip quickly out the door.
Will 4 baskets hold all their apples?
Absolutely! Sure!

5 pudgy pigeons follow Ernie and Bert. And Ernie's Rubber Duckie gives **5** squeaks and a squirt.

SQUEAK!
SQUEAK!
SQUEAK!
SQUEAK!
SQUEAK!

6 batty bats have come to lend a hand.
The Count laughs, "*Ah, ah, ah!*" **6** times.
"Apple counting's grand!"

7 fairy frogs and sweet Abby join the crowd. "Apples are enchanting," she and the **7** sing aloud.

8 tiny Twiddlebugs want to share the fun.
All **8** ride in Big Bird's wagon—
every single one!

9 hungry squirrels share Cookie's crunchy snack. Cookie says, "So yummy! Me and all **9** coming back!"

10 tasty treats for all, **10** apples ripe and sweet to eat. What a sunny, yummy day for our friends on Sesame Street!

COUNTING ALL AROUND

One, two, three, four, five, six, seven, and eight and nine and ten!

Zoe knows numbers are special,
but *especially* special when . . .

she counts ten invitations
to a great big birthday bash.
She's got to mail them all today,
so Zoe has to dash!

Now Zoe's at the post office.
What else can she count there?
Outside there's **one** blue mailbox.
Are there **two** steps anywhere?

POST OFFICE

2

Rosita mails **three** letters
to her *familia* far away.

Baby Bear sees **four** mail slots.
Which one will he use today?

Here

There

Near

Far

4

5

There are already
five in line.
Zoe gets on the end.

Grover delivers **six** postcards.
(He's not a mailman—it's just pretend.)

Big Bird has **seven** packages.
That's quite a stack to mail.

Elmo helps! He adds one box—
all **eight** go on the scale.

Zoe already has one stamp.
She needs **nine** more today.

Ten invitations for her friends.
Bye-bye! They're on their way!

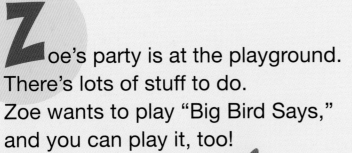

Zoe's party is at the playground.
There's lots of stuff to do.
Zoe wants to play "Big Bird Says,"
and you can play it, too!

"Big Bird says . . . begin with **1** spin."
Zoe twirls right around.

"Big Bird says . . . now do **2** jumps."
Elmo bounces up and down.

"Big Bird says . . .
pat your head **3** times."

Baby Bear pats:
one, two, three!

"Big Bird says . . . let's do **4** hops.
Please hop along with me."

"Big Bird says . . . do **5** toe touches. S t r e t c h and touch your toesies!"

"Big Bird says . . . let's do **6** nose rubs. Reach up and rub your nosies!"

"Now do **7** jumping jacks."

Uh-oh! What did Big Bird forget to say?

"Big Bird says . . . do **8** shoulder taps."
Now that's the way to play!

"Big Bird says . . . do **9** tummy rubs."
Cookie loves this part the best.

"Big Bird says . . . now clap **10** times."
Let's applaud our special guest!

Zoe loves her party.
She counted on friends to make it fun.
Guess who made it **ten** times nicer?
You guessed it! You're the **one**!

THE COUNT'S CASTLE

"What a wonderful day for a counting party!" thought Elmo, as he stopped by 123 Sesame Street to meet his friends Bert, Ernie, and Zoe. They were all invited to the Count's Castle that day, and Elmo couldn't wait to start counting.

Eager to be on his way, Elmo looked out the window and saw a little black puppy.

"One! One cute puppy!" Elmo counted.

"Come on everyone! Elmo doesn't want to be late for the party," Elmo called to Bert, Ernie, and Zoe. "It's time to go-go-go!"

"Greetings and welcome to my Counting Party!"
said the Count to his friends.

Elmo, Zoe, Bert, and Ernie were so excited to begin.
They never noticed another guest slip inside the door.

"After we find everything on my list, we will celebrate
with cupcakes," said the Count. "Let the counting begin!

"I found the first thing," said Zoe. "One Countmobile!"
"ONE!" counted the Count. "Wonderful, wonderful!"
"I see the two portraits," said Ernie.
"TWO!" said the Count. "Two grinning grandparents!"

"We need to find three green capes in a closet,"
said Zoe.
"I see them!" said Bert.

"THREE!" counted the Count. "How I love to count my lovely capes!"

"Four suits of armor!" said Elmo.

"FOUR!" said the Count. "Let's keep counting."

"You know, black cats aren't scary at all," said Ernie.
"1, 2, 3, 4, 5," counted Zoe. "Five adorable black kitties."
"FIVE!" shouted the Count. "Let's count some more!"

"Six lightning bolts!" said Ernie as the evening sky lit up outside the kitchen window.

"SIX!" said the Count. "I love the number six."

"Elmo sees seven bats," said Elmo.
"SEVEN!" said the Count. "Seven
beautiful batty bats!"

"There are the eight spiders," said Bert. "EIGHT!" said the Count happily. "Eight splendid spiders!"

"Does anybody see the nine keys?" asked Zoe.
"I do!" said Bert.
"NINE!" counted the Count. "Fantastic!"
"Now we just need to find ten balloons and we can eat!" said Ernie. "Does anybody see them?"

The Count just smiled. Where could those balloons be?

"1, 2, 3, 4, 5, 6, 7, 8, 9, 10! There they are!" called Elmo.
"TEN!" shouted the Count. "Ah-ah-aaah! It's time to eat!"
Everyone gathered around the table to sing "Happy
Counting to You" to the Count.

When the party was over, everyone thanked the Count and said good-bye.

"Farewell!" said the Count. "Good-bye to my four wonderful counting friends."

But how many friends do *you* count? Ah-ah-aah!

THE END